First published 1993
by Walker Books Ltd
87 Vauxhall Walk, London SE11 5HJ

This edition published 2007

2 4 6 8 10 9 7 5 3 1

Printed in China

British Library Cataloguing in Publication Data:
a catalogue record for this book
is available from the British Library

ISBN 978-1-4063-1077-1

www.walkerbooks.co.uk

HIDE AND SEEK

Jez Alborough

WALKER BOOKS

AND SUBSIDIARIES

LONDON · BOSTON · SYDNEY · AUCKLAND

I'm Frog.
I'm playing hide and seek
with my friends,

but I can't see anyone.
Can you?

I'm playing hide and seek
with my friends,

but Hippo and I
can't see anyone.
Can you?

I'm playing hide and seek
with my friends,

but Hippo, Snake and I
can't see anyone.
Can you?

I'm playing hide and seek
with my friends,

but Hippo, Snake, Tortoise
and I can't see anyone.
Can you?

I'm playing hide and seek
with my friends,

but Hippo, Snake, Tortoise, Toucan and I can't see anyone. Can you?

Now where's Frog?
We can't see him anywhere.
Can you?

WALKER BOOKS is the world's leading
independent publisher of children's books.
Working with the best authors and illustrators
we create books for all ages, from babies
to teenagers – books your child will
grow up with and always remember. So…

FOR THE BEST CHILDREN'S BOOKS,
LOOK FOR THE BEAR

THIS WALKER BOOK BELONGS TO:

_____

_____

_____